WHAT AM I?

WHAT AM I?

An Animal Guessing Game

by Iza Trapani

Whispering Coyote Press, Inc.
1992
New York

Published by Whispering Coyote Press Inc.
P.O. Box 2159, Halesite, New York 11743-2159
Copyright © 1992 by Iza Trapani
All rights reserved including the right of
reproduction in whole or in part in any form.
Printed in Hong Kong by South China Printing Company (1988) Ltd.
Book production and design by Our House

CIP data is available upon request.
ISBN 1-879085-76-3

To my family and friends—
thanks for believing in me.
                                    —I.T.

Let's play a game. Let's have some fun.
Guess the animals one by one.
They'll give you hints to help you win.
Get ready, set, and let's begin!

My neck is long. My wings are short.
They tell me I'm an awkward sort.
And when I hear a scary sound,
I hide my head deep in the ground.
Perhaps you'd like to hide with me.
That would be fun, don't you agree?

What am I?

An Ostrich!

I'm just as wide as I am tall.
My ears are small, but that is all.
I wade in rivers all day long.
Some say I'm ugly, but they're wrong.
I think that I'm a handsome chap.
May I please sit down in your lap?

What am I?

A Hippopotamus!

My yellow eyes are big and round.
At night I make a hooting sound.
I sleep all day high in a tree,
So please try not to bother me.
But if I see you home at night,
Then I'll stop by, if that's all right.

What am I?

An Owl!

I live where there is always snow.
Up north where cold winds often blow.
My fur is white and very thick.
I see a fish; I snag it quick.
Perhaps you'd like to dine with me.
I'll cook the fish, you make the tea.

What am I?

A Polar Bear!

My home is on the ocean coast,
And swimming is what I like most.
I have brown fur that gleams and glows,
And splendid whiskers on my nose.
They say I'm nice, and yes, it's true.
I'll clap my flippers just for you!

What am I?

A Seal!

I'm not especially fast, you know.
In fact, I'm told I'm truly slow.
But I can hide inside my shell.
And that, I think, is simply swell.
I'd love to join you for a hike,
But I'm too slow. Let's ride a bike.

What am I?

A Turtle!

My coat is red and silky, too.
I like my bushy tail, don't you?
They say I'm sly; don't ask me why.
I think that I'm a decent guy.
Perhaps you'd like to visit me,
And see how charming I can be.

What am I?

A Fox!

I live in jungles full of weeds.
I like to munch on roots and seeds.
If you disturb me while I rest,
I might stand up and beat my chest.
But I'm quite gentle, you will see.
Why don't you come and play with me?

What am I?

A Gorilla!

My home is in a hot, dry land,
And there I walk the desert sand.
I have a hump that's really neat,
And two big toes on all my feet.
Hop on my back, it's quite all right.
It could be bumpy; hold on tight!

What am I?

A Camel!

I'm very sloppy, so they say.
I roll around in mud all day.
I'm rather heavy for my size.
I've gained some weight, I realize.
But though I'm fat, I need love, too.
Let's cuddle up, just me and you!

What am I?

A Pig!

Well, that was fun, my little one,
But now this guessing game is done.
And since there's nothing left to do,
Let's snuggle up, just me and you!